For my parents, who happily washed the mud off after childhood adventures, and for all the little people yet to discover the joy...

A.J.

For Mum and Dad, for lovely childhood memories and our brown cows...

A.S.

The Mackenzie family ♡ x x

Mum Elin

Dad Fraser

Tim

Suzie

Eve

Dudley
and the
Secret Walk

by

Annette Stacey

Illustrated by

Alison Johnston

Dudley was a dog who lived in a big house, with a big garden to run around in, and a family who loved him very much. He was a very happy dog.

Dudley loved going for walks with his family. Out of the gate and down the lane, across the wooden bridge and into the field. Dad would throw sticks and Suzie and Tim would have a race with Dudley to see who could get the stick first. Dudley would always win.

"What time are we going for a walk today?" asked Tim.
Dudley looked at Dad hopefully.
"At 4 o'clock," replied Dad.
"Why do we have to wait?" thought Dudley crossly.
He went to lie in his basket and very soon he fell asleep.

The big clock in the hall chimed. One, two, three...

Dudley walked into the kitchen.

He had heard the words, "Granny and Grandpa" and "Tea" mentioned and Mum had been rushing around.

"Out!" cried Mum.
"It's only 3 o'clock. I still have lots to do. And please don't walk on the wet floor Dudley or I will need to start again."

Dudley went to find Dad. He was in his office. Dudley looked at Dad hopefully. "It's a bit early," said Dad looking at his watch. "I've still got lots to do. We will go later, Dudley, I promise."

Dudley walked sadly to the sitting room and peeped in. The new baby was asleep in her pram. Perhaps if the new baby was awake, they could all go for their walk. Everybody always stopped what they were doing when Eve was awake.

...he barked
quietly...

...he barked
a bit louder...

"WO..." He started.

"Dudley!" Mum pulled him out of the room. "Please be a good dog. I am very busy today."

Dudley crept up the stairs and looked in Tim's room. There was a huge racing car track that covered the floor. Dudley sat down, right in front of two little cars that were whizzing round. "Oh Dudley," sighed Tim, "Please can you move, I will have to start again now."

Dudley could hear the sound of music coming from Suzie's room. She was dancing and she didn't see Dudley until it was too late.

CRASH

"Oh Dudley," sighed Suzie.

"I have to do it all again now."

"All I want to do is go for a walk," thought Dudley. "If nobody will take me then I will go by myself."

Out into the garden he went. Dudley leapt
over the wall and landed in the lane.

Dudley walked over the wooden bridge that
would take him to his favourite field. "What a
great adventure, this is a lovely walk," thought
Dudley. He looked up. "Oh no," he shivered.

There was the boy from next door with his grumpy dog, Brady. Brady stared at Dudley and he growled softly. Then Brady growled a bit louder. He was getting closer and closer. Dudley had to get away.

He jumped into the hedge and squeezed through the brambles to the other side.

But he wasn't in his favourite field; he was on the main road! Suddenly BEEP! BEEP! A car whooshed past. Dudley felt very scared. He knew the road was dangerous. "Oh thank goodness, there is a gate," he thought. He quickly ran underneath it.

Only he still wasn't in his favourite field. He was in
a field full of brown and white cows. They didn't look
very pleased to see him. They walked slowly towards
him and then they started to run. Dudley ran too,
as fast as he could towards the corner of the field and
squeezed under a fence.

Dudley thought, "I'm not enjoying my walk. There is nobody to play with, nobody to run with and nobody to throw me sticks. I don't like grumpy dogs, fast cars and scary cows. I don't like going on adventures by myself." Then he thought, "what way is home?"
He felt very sorry for himself.

Suddenly he heard a familiar sound, it was Dad whistling for him. Dudley ran as fast as he could.

Dad didn't look very happy. "Uh-Oh!" thought Dudley. "Home," said Dad crossly.

When they got home everybody was waiting for them.
"Oh Dudley," said Mum, "you must never go off for
a walk by yourself. You could have got lost or hurt."
"You frightened us," said Dad, "you must never do
that again." Suzie and Tim didn't say anything. They
were too busy giving Dudley a great big hug. Even
baby Eve smiled at him.

The big clock in the hall started to chime.
One, two, three, four! Dudley looked at Dad.
"Alright," smiled Dad...

"but this time we
will all go together."

How To Organise The Perfect Walk

You might need...

1) Waterproof boots - good for splashing in puddles.

2) Umbrella - useful in case it rains or to use as a sunshade.

3) A bag - in case you find treasures like feathers, leaves and flowers, or to collect blackberries.

4) A note book and pencil - to draw a map!

5) A magnifying glass - to look closely at creatures, insects, plants or paw prints.

6) A ball, frisbee or stick - to play games.

7) A dog - if you haven't got one perhaps a friend has!

8) A grown up - remember it's much more fun to go for a walk with other people that you know.

9) A tasty snack - especially on long walks. Can you help to make a picnic?

10) Don't forget your Camera!

This story can be used to encourage child development in relation to the seven areas of Early Years Curriculum.

Teaching Aid for 'Dudley and the Secret Walk'

Communication and Language

1)   Talk about how we can do things to help our friends and family. Talk about families and pets and bring in favourite photos.

2)   Talk about the importance of looking after our pets, and how important it is to take dogs and ourselves for healthy walks.

Literacy

1)   Read the story of ' Dudley and the Secret Walk'. Talk about what is seen and what is happening in the illustrations

2)   Can the Children sound out the expressive words in the story like 'WOOF', 'CRASH', 'BEEP BEEP' etc and have a go at writing Them.

Personal, Social and Emotional Development

1)   Encourage the children to talk about feelings i.e. happy, sad, angry, jealous etc.

2)   Talk about the importance of sharing, taking turns, waiting patiently. Play games that encourage the children to do this.

3)   Explain about the importance of road safety and of going for a walk with people you know and not by yourself.

Knowledge and Understanding of the World

1) Encourage the children to look at the different clocks in the story and to talk about the clocks they have at home.

2) Encourage the children to go for walks and to bring in to Nursery/School the treasures they have found – feathers, leaves, flowers etc.

3) Make an interest table with the things they find on their walks or in their gardens.

4) Encourage the children to bring in photos of different places they have visited and make a display.

5) The cows in the pictures are called 'Ayrshires' and are from Scotland. Encourage the children to look at different breeds of cows.

Mathematical Development

1) Teach the children about time. Encourage them to look at the different clocks in the story and to see what time each one says.

2) Count objects in the story. How many clocks are there? How many cows are there? Etc.

3) Teach the children how to play 'What's the time Mr Wolf?' (Counting footsteps).

Physical Development

1) Encourage the children to take part in activities that incorporate running, jumping, dancing, climbing etc.

2) Take the children for seasonal walks, spring, summer, autumn, winter. Invite parents/carers to come with you.

3) Encourage the children to dress themselves in the appropriate clothing for seasons – gloves, scarves, wellies, hats, coats for autumn/winter. Sunhats/sun cream for summer etc.

4) Play 'Sleepy Lions' or 'Sleepy Dudley' with the children.

Expressive arts and Design

1) Encourage the children to pretend to be different animals including Dudley.

2) Pretend to be clocks and design and make a model of a clock.

3) Encourage the children to make collage pictures or crowns with the things they have found on their walk i.e. using flowers, feathers etc.

4) Encourage the children to draw/paint pictures of Dudley and to write and talk about their favourite part of the story.

5) In the story Granny and Grandpa are coming for tea. Have a tea party at school and encourage the children to invite their grandparents. Perhaps the children could design and write invitations and make cakes.

Annette Stacey

Annette Stacey has lived in Somerset all her life. She trained at Bridgwater College for her NNEB Qualification and has worked as a private Nanny. She now owns and runs a Pre-School Nursery Group in Street, Somerset. Annette has been inspired by the children she has worked with over the years and she has written several articles which have appeared in magazines.
'Dudley and the Secret Walk' is the second of her many children's stories to be published.

Alison Johnston

Award winning artist Alison Johnston trained at the Edinburgh College of Art. She now lives in Moray, Scotland after having lived in Somerset for many years. She has achieved great success in animation with children's television programmes such as 'Fireman Sam'. Alison is a professional artist and she exhibits her work from her studio in Scotland and Art Exhibitions. Alison was thrilled to be given artistic freedom to design the Dudley books.

Dudley and the Chocolate Birthday Cake

'Dudley and the Chocolate Birthday Cake' is the first in the series of the Dudley books and was published in 2007. It is a much loved story about a dog who can't resist the smell of a delicious birthday cake and thinks that if he had a little bit nobody would notice... or would they! There is also a teaching plan, colouring sheet and recipe idea to accompany this story.

You can follow Dudley on his own Facebook page 'Dudley and the Chocolate Birthday Cake'

https://www.facebook.com/Dudley-and-the-Chocolate-Birthday-Cake-238931649475531